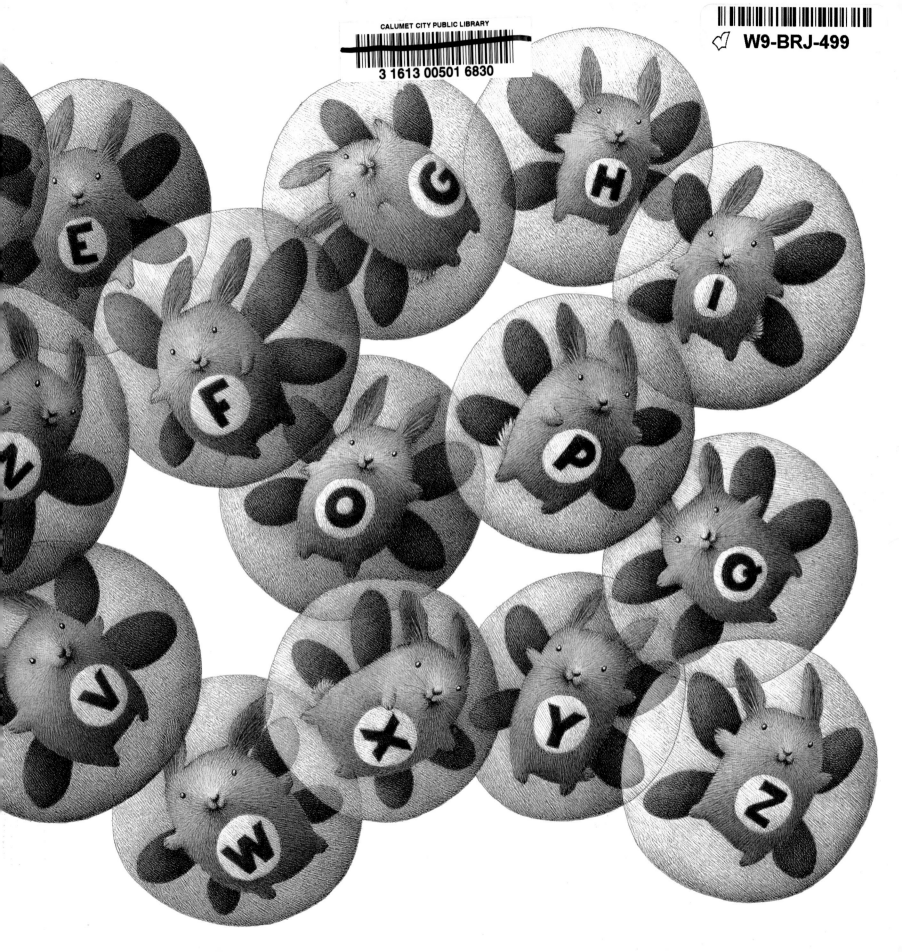

Henry Holt and Company, LLC
Publishers since 1866
175 Fifth Avenue
New York, New York 10010
mackids.com

Library of Congress Cataloging-in-Publication Data
McCarty, Peter, author, illustrator.
Bunny dreams / Peter McCarty. — First edition.
pages cm
Summary: "In bunny dreams, anything can happen. A bunny might know the A-B-Cs,
or count by 1-2-3s. A bunny might find the perfect carrot. A bunny might hop, hop, hop,
or even fly! But every bunny needs a cozy place to rest"—Provided by publisher.
ISBN 978-0-8050-9687-3 (hardback)
[1. Rabbits—Fiction. 2. Bedtime—Fiction.] I. Title.
PZ7.M47841327Bu 2016   [E]—dc23   2015009202

Henry Holt books may be purchased for business or promotional use. For
information on bulk purchases, please contact the Macmillan Corporate
and Premium Sales Department at (800) 221-7945 x5442 or by e-mail at
specialmarkets@macmillan.com.

First Edition—2016 / Designed by Patrick Collins
Printed in China by RR Donnelley Asia Printing Solutions Ltd.,
Dongguan City, Guangdong Province

1 3 5 7 9 10 8 6 4 2

BUNNY DREAMS

PETER McCARTY

Henry Holt and Company
New York

Look at all the bunnies
hopping all around.

What do bunnies know?

Bunnies know to eat their vegetables—
although they do not know their names.

Bunnies know to run from the farmer's dog—
even if he only wants to play.

Bunnies know when it's time to rest.
They know they need a place to hide.

There are tunnels underground
where bunnies are safe—
safe to sleep and dream.

Where do bunnies go
when they dream?

They fly into the air with bees and butterflies....

They float up
and over a big blue dog. . . .

They know
their A-B-Cs
and 1-2-3s. . . .

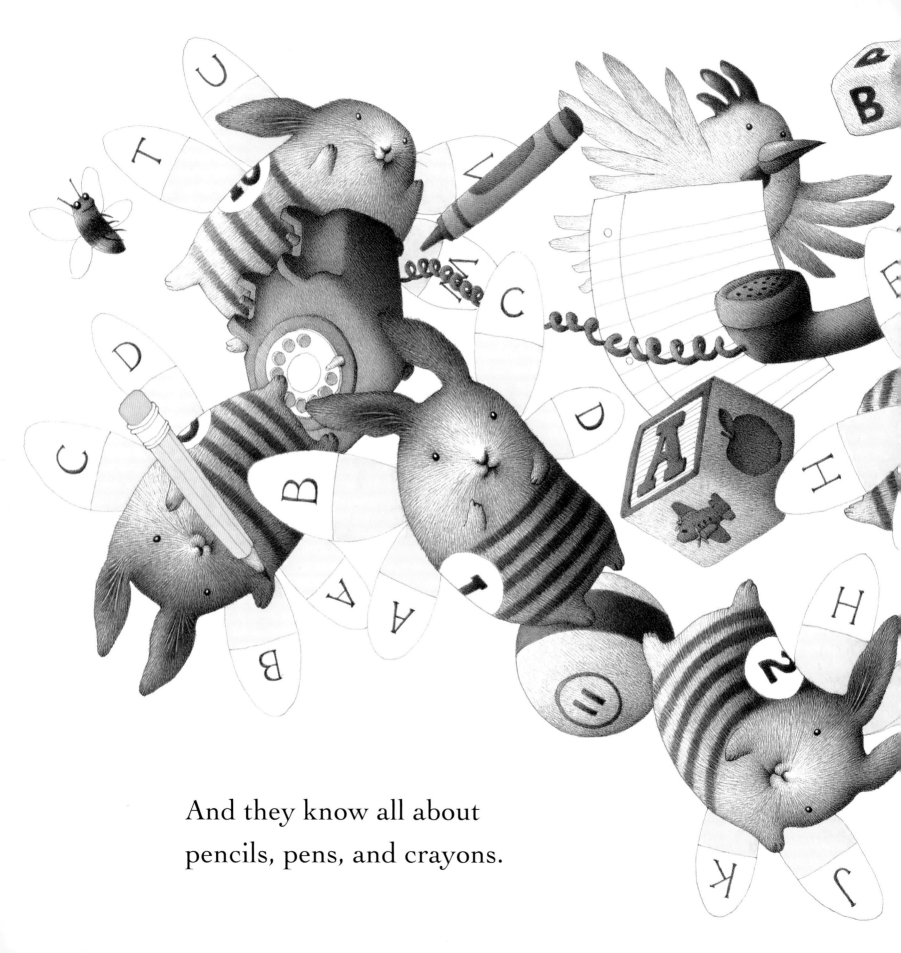

And they know all about
pencils, pens, and crayons.

Brenda, Bobby, Brian, Bridget, Bonnie,
Billy, Ben, Betty, Brandon, and Beth . . .

Bunnies know how to write their names,
but only in their dreams.

Sometimes one bunny will say, "This is not what I know. I am a bunny, and my name is not Bobby!"

Then that bunny
will wake up . . .

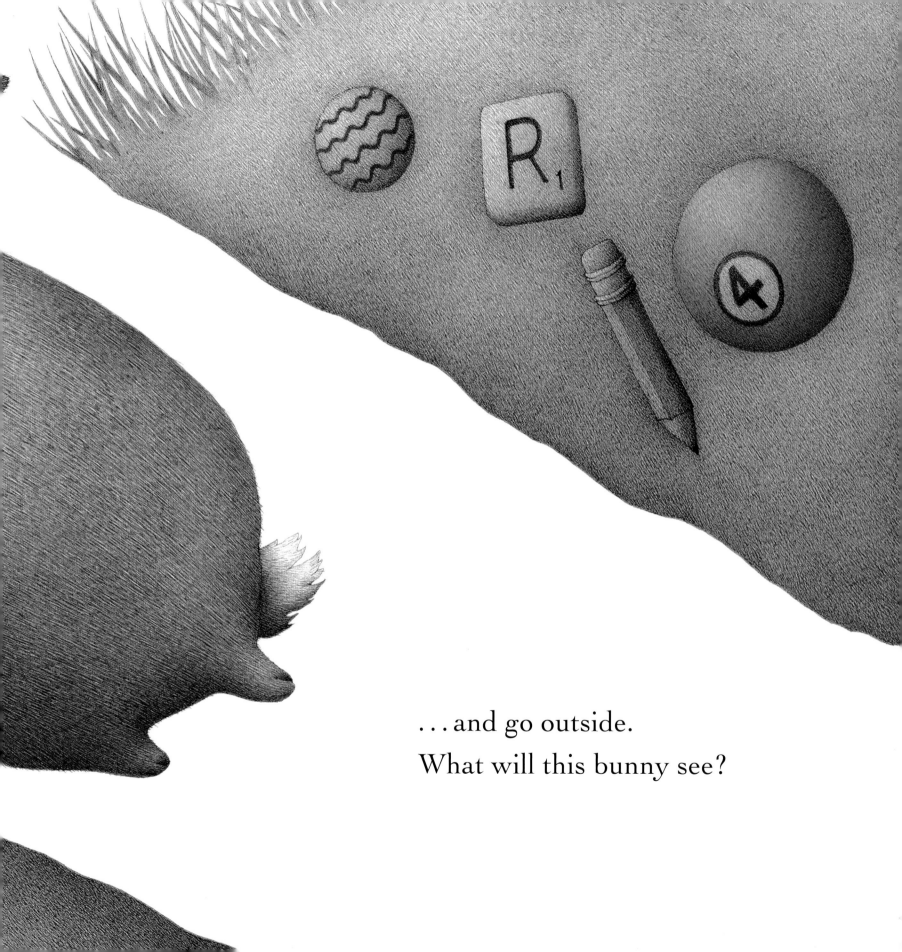

...and go outside.
What will this bunny see?

He will see something shining
and round,
something magical!

Is it another Bunny Dream?

No. It is real. It is the moon.

And all the bunnies will stop their dreaming
and hop outside
to see the bunny on the moon.

Can you see it, too?

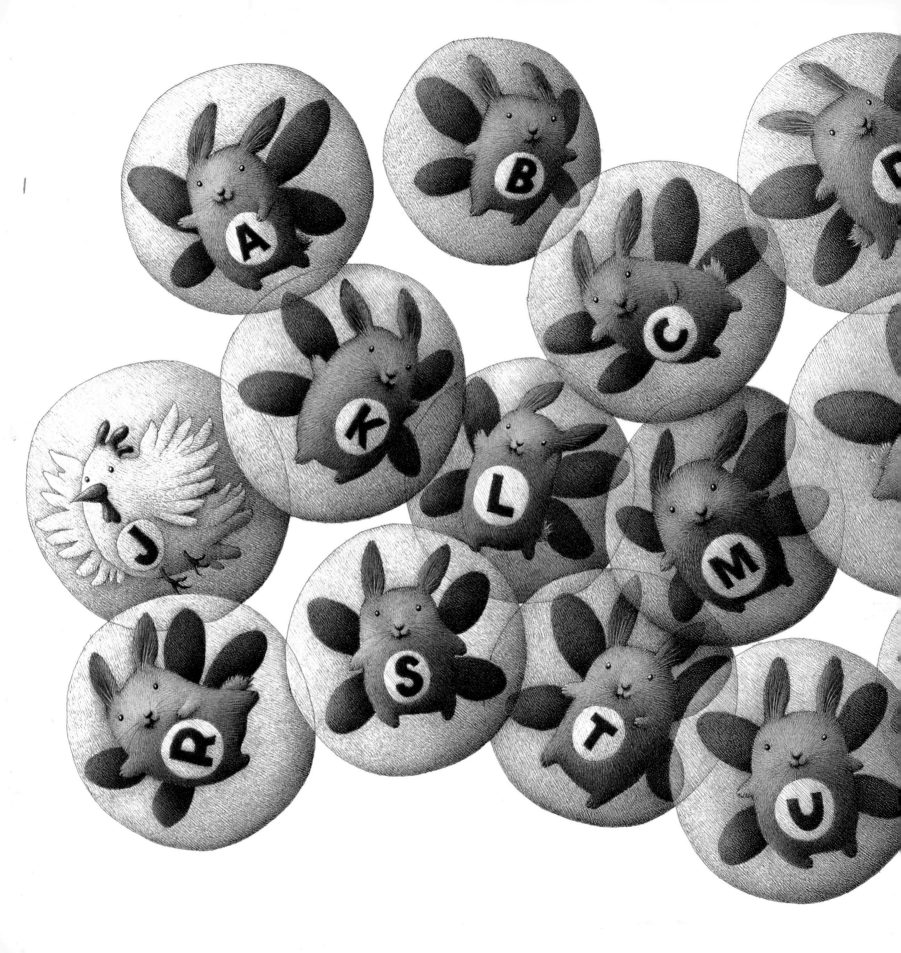